Young Cousins Mysteries™
The Chalk Drawings Mystery

P9-CCT-300

by Elspeth Campbell Murphy
Illustrated by Nancy Munger

Timothy Sarah-Jane Titus

*A trustworthy messenger
refreshes those who send him.
He is like the coolness of snow in the summertime.*

Proverbs 25:13

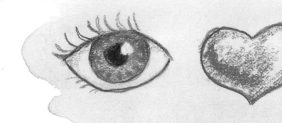

The Chalk Drawings Mystery
Copyright © 2002
Elspeth Campbell Murphy

Cover and story illustrations by Nancy Munger
Cover design by Jennifer Parker

YOUNG COUSINS MYSTERIES is a trademark of Elspeth Campbell Murphy.

Scripture quotation is from the *International Children's Bible, New Century Version,* copyright © 1986, 1988 by Word Publishing, Dallas, Texas 75039. Used by permission.

Published by Bethany House Publishers
A Ministry of Bethany Fellowship International
11400 Hampshire Avenue South
Bloomington, Minnesota 55438
www.bethanyhouse.com

Printed in China.

Library of Congress Catalog-in-Publication Data

CIP data applied for

ISBN 0-7642-2497-2

Contents

Chapter One
The Strange Drawings

Timothy Dawson loved to draw.
And he was very good at it.

"EX-cellent robots, Tim!"
said his cousin Titus.

The robots were chalk drawings
Timothy had made on the sidewalk
in front of his school.

Timothy took special art classes
at school in the summertime.

"I drew them yesterday," said Timothy.
"My teacher, Miss Mattie, will see them
when she comes to school today."

Other children had left pictures
for Miss Mattie, too.

"Who made these birds?"
asked Timothy's cousin Sarah-Jane.

"Probably Jessica," said Timothy.
"She's Miss Mattie's niece."

"Jessica's drawings are good,"
said Sarah-Jane.

"Yes," agreed Timothy.
"But Jessica doesn't like it
when Miss Mattie says that
other kids' drawings are good, too."

QX WILL XX QYOU XX MARRY XQME QX?

Suddenly, Timothy noticed
some other drawings.

They were a little apart from the rest.

Timothy frowned.

They hadn't been there
yesterday afternoon.

Titus and Sarah-Jane came over to see.

"Nice drawings!" said Sarah-Jane.

"Did you do them, Tim?" asked Titus.

"Not me," said Timothy.

"I'm good. But I'm not *that* good. *No* kid is *that* good. I think a *grown-up* made these pictures."

Chapter Two
Whose Drawings?

Sarah-Jane and Titus looked at Tim in surprise.

"Why would a *grown-up* draw on the sidewalk?" asked Sarah-Jane.

Titus added, "It would look pretty odd if anyone saw him!"

Timothy shrugged.

"Maybe he did it at night, when no one was around."

"But how could he see?" asked Titus. "It would be hard to hold a flashlight and draw at the same time."

"This person didn't need a flashlight," said Timothy. "Look!"

He pointed up.

Sarah-Jane and Titus looked up.

"Aha!" said Titus. "A streetlight!"

"OK," said Sarah-Jane slowly.
"We're guessing that a grown-up
made these drawings.
He drew them at night
under a streetlight.
But that still doesn't tell us *why*.
Why would a grown-up
draw on the sidewalk?"

Timothy took a little notebook and pencil out of his pocket.

(He always carried these around in case he wanted to draw something.)

"It looks like a puzzle," he said as he copied it down.

"It's got question marks around it. I wonder what it means."

"It looks like a letter," said Titus.
"See? There's a picture of a deer.
It could stand for the word *Dear*."

"Right!" said Sarah-Jane.
"And then there's a picture of a mat.
Plus an e. . . . *'Dear Mattie'!*"

They looked at the end of the letter
to see who it was from.

"What's that?" asked Timothy.
"A cup of *coffee*? What kind of sense
does *that* make?"

"My dad always calls it
a cup of joe," said Titus.

The cousins looked at one another.

A secret letter to Timothy's teacher
from someone named Joe?

Chapter Three
What Happened?

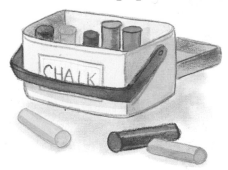

Timothy said,
"I have a puzzle book at home.
Maybe we can use it
to figure out *this* puzzle."

"I don't know about that,"
said Sarah-Jane.

"You're not supposed to read
other people's mail, you know."

"The sidewalk isn't mail," said Titus.

"Sure, this is a letter.
But it didn't come in a sealed envelope
from the mailman."

"It's still mail," said Sarah-Jane.

"No, it isn't," said Titus.

"Yes, it is," said Sarah-Jane.

"No, it isn't," said Titus.

They argued about this
all the way back to Timothy's house—
and all the way back to school.

But when they got back to school,
the argument didn't matter anymore.

That's because the beautiful puzzle
was gone.

The cousins blinked.

They hadn't *imagined* it, had they?

But no.

The sidewalk was wet.

Someone had washed away the chalk.

Wet footprints led to a girl
who was sitting on the grass nearby.

She had a bucket of colored chalk.
And she was busily adding
to her bird picture.

"Jessica," said Timothy. "What happened
to the chalk puzzle?"

Jessica did not look up.

She tried to slip something
behind her back.

But she was not fast enough.

Sarah-Jane grabbed the thing.

It was a wet sponge.

"Jessica!" yelled Timothy.
"Why did you wash off the puzzle?"

Jessica looked about to cry.
"Because! Your puzzle was so pretty.
I knew Aunt Mattie would like it better
than my birds!"

"It wasn't *my* puzzle!" said Timothy.
"It was a secret message from someone
named *Joe*!"

Jessica gulped. "Uh-oh!"

Chapter Four
The Secret Message

"Who's Joe?" asked Titus.

"My aunt's boyfriend," said Jessica.

"Uh-oh," said Sarah-Jane.

"What am I going to do?" wailed Jessica.

"I know I have to tell her what I did. And that I'm sorry. But the message is gone, gone, gone!"

"No, it isn't," said Timothy.

"Yes, it is," said Jessica.

"No, it isn't," said Timothy.

He pulled the notebook out of his pocket.

Timothy found a dry spot
on the sidewalk.

He borrowed a piece of Jessica's chalk.

Then he carefully copied the puzzle
from his notebook.

It didn't look as good
as the first puzzle, of course.

But it still looked pretty good.

While Timothy was working,
the cousins and Jessica couldn't help
trying to figure it out.

Sarah-Jane said,
"The picture of the eye could mean *I*.
And the picture of the heart
could mean *love*."

"But what about the sheep?" asked
Titus. "'I love *sheep*'?
What kind of sense does *that* make?"

Jessica suddenly yelled,
"'I love *you*'!"

"Ex-*cuse* me?" said Titus.

Jessica sighed impatiently.
"A lady sheep is called a *ewe*.
It sounds the same as *you*.
But it's not spelled the same.
Spelling doesn't matter for a picture."

Titus shrugged. "Makes sense,
I guess."

"Of course it does," said Sarah-Jane.
"Now, what about the rest?
There are no pictures there."

Timothy flipped through his puzzle
book.

"Sometimes you can find a message
by taking out the extra letters," he said.

"Nobody uses the letters *Q* and *X*
very much . . ." said Titus.

So Jessica took her sponge
and very, very carefully
erased the letters *Q* and *X*.

WILL YOU MARRY ME ?

They gathered round to read
the secret message.
"Uh-oh," said Jessica.

Chapter Five
Hearts and Flowers

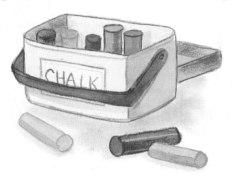

"Uh-oh," said Jessica again. "I guess that was a pretty important message, wasn't it?"

"That's why Joe drew all those pretty pictures around it," said Sarah-Jane.

Jessica and the cousins looked at one another.

The pictures!

They had the puzzle, all right.

But it looked so plain without the beautiful chalk drawings around it.

Jessica shared her chalk.

Then she and the cousins got to work.

They drew hearts and flowers

and question marks around the puzzle.

They were so busy drawing
that they didn't hear Miss Mattie
come up behind them.

It took a while to explain
everything that had happened.

As soon as Miss Mattie understood,
she ran into the school to call Joe.

Jessica sighed.

"It's supposed to rain tonight," she said.

"It *is*?" squeaked Timothy.
"What about our chalk drawings?
They'll all get washed away!"

"Wait here!" said Jessica.

She ran across the street to her house.

And came back with a camera.

Miss Mattie used Jessica's camera to take pictures of Timothy's robots and Jessica's birds and all the other children's drawings.

But mostly she took pictures of the important secret message.

She said it was
the most beautiful thing she had ever seen.

WILL YOU MARRY ME?

The End

MG